To Penelope Farmer, my best source.
And to makers of all kinds T. M.

For Louis J. L.

WAYLAND
A DAVID FICKLING BOOK 978 0 85756014 8

Published in Great Britain by David Fickling Books,
a division of Random House Children's Publishers UK
A Random House Group Company

This edition published 2013

1 3 5 7 9 10 8 6 4 2

Set in Atma Serif-Book Roman

DAVID FICKLING BOOKS
31 Beaumont Street, Oxford, OX1 2NP

www.**randomhousechildrens**.co.uk
www.**totallyrandombooks**.co.uk
www.**randomhouse**.co.uk

Addresses for companies within The Random House Group Limited can be found at: www.randomhouse.co.uk/offices.htm

THE RANDOM HOUSE GROUP Limited Reg. No. 954009

A CIP catalogue record for this book is available from the British Library.

Printed in China.

WAYLAND

WAYLAND

TONY MITTON

ILLUSTRATED BY
JOHN LAWRENCE

David Fickling Books

OUT OF THE LANDS in the chill, far north
come legends from long ago.
This is the story of Wayland Smith,
the strangest of all I know.

For out of the dark spring stories
to banish both drear and cold.
So gather you near, come, listen and hear,
where the fire burns red and gold.

There once lived a band of three brothers
where the bears and the wolf packs roam.
Three Swan–Maidens dwelt with those brothers,
as wives in their woodland home.

Two of the brothers were Warriors,
deft in the hunt and the kill.
But the third was the sturdy smith, Wayland,
a Maker of marvellous skill.

The brothers brought meat to the table
and battled, for gold, in the wars.
But Wayland the Smith, though the strongest,
stayed close to his craft, indoors.

And though he was different, they loved him,
admiring the things that he made.
He protected the home in their absence,
and his work brought a comfortable trade.

Wayland the Maker wrought weapons
of magical temper and power,
and wonderful shields and chain-metal shirts
to ward off the arrow shower.

And also he fashioned adornments
of glistening silver and gold,
necklaces, earrings and armbands,
bright wonders for folk to behold.

For, although he was massive and awkward,
his making was second to none.
And those who came seeking his craftskill
would gasp when the work was done.

The brothers of Wayland went hunting.
They brought back the deer and the bear.
But Wayland the Maker stayed close to his forge
and fashioned things fierce and things fair.

The Swan-Sisters tended the dwelling.
They baked, and they swept out the hearth.
They gathered wild herbs and sweet berries
that grew by the side of the path.

It is said you lay claim to a Swan-Bride
by concealing her feathery cape.
Without it she cannot change back to a bird
to return to the air and escape.

The warrior brothers had chanced on the Maids
as they bathed on a hot summer's day.
They'd spotted the swan-capes laid out on the bank
and they'd seized them and stashed them away.

And as the Maids stepped from the water,
the brothers had claimed them as wives,
"So long as your capes remain hidden
you must stay with us all of our lives."

Two of the Swan–Maids were haughty
and their beauty could strike like a thrill.
But the third sister, Alvit, was plainer.
She was quiet and simple and still.

"Wayland!" cried out his two brothers,
as they came to their dwelling that night,
"We have brought you the Swan–Maiden, Alvit.
May she bring you both luck and delight."

So Wayland agreed to take Alvit
and the two seemed to suit one another.
And as for her sisters so haughty,
there was one for each warrior brother.

The brothers had hidden the Swan–Sisters' capes
in a chest, in a cave below ground.
They knew that they'd have to remain, as their wives,
so long as the capes were not found.

But one day, out searching for berries,
the Swan–Sisters chanced on the chest.
In no time their sinewy bodies
with snowy white feathers were dressed.

Two of the Sisters were swift to escape
and they called as they rose on the breeze.
But Alvit, the fair wife of Wayland,
went straight to his forge in the trees.

Often she'd watched him, intent on his work,
making a brooch or a ring.
But out of all gifts that he'd fashioned for her
she'd only accepted one thing:

An armband both simple and graceful
with a delicate sketch of a feather.
It stood for her wedding to Wayland
and their life in the forest together.

Although she was captive, she loved him
for his kindness and courteous ways.
There was richness and warmth in his workshop
and dependable love in his gaze.

Wayland looked up from his furnace
to see his wife's shape in the door.
And he knew all at once she was leaving,
from the feathery cape that she wore.

"I am leaving," said Alvit to Wayland,
"for my home in the vault of the sky.
I was happy enough as your partner,
so I come here to bid you goodbye.

"You gave me your care and your kindness.
You kept out the cold and the rain.
Who knows, but that one day, in heaven,
we two may be partners again?"

The armband she dropped at the threshold
as she shifted her shape to a swan.
She looked at him sadly and softly,
then spread out her wings and was gone.

Wayland made straight for the doorway,
as he let out a sorrowful sigh.
He watched while his simple, young Swan–Bride
flew off in the vast of the sky.

His warrior brothers came running.
They'd seen the three swans fly away.
They determined to search to the ends of the earth
and bring back their brides one day.

But Wayland refused to go with them.
His decision was solid as stone.
He'd stay at his forge and continue his work,
and live in the forest alone.

A Swan-Maid belongs in the heaven
to ferry the souls of the dead.
While a Maker like Wayland belongs at his forge
to bring forth the things from his head.

Fate had brought Alvit to Wayland
and fate would now take her away.
It was useless to question such workings.
There was nothing to do or to say.

So Wayland went back to his furnace
as his brothers set off on their quest.
But he secretly hoped she'd return in the end
to her Wayland, who loved her the best.

So before he went back to his labours
he hung up her band by the door,
as a token to say that forever he'd pray
for the fall of her foot on his floor.

Wayland stayed close to his furnace,
but his fame as a maker spread wide.
And folk were amazed at the wares that he made.
But he never had word of his bride.

Not far from the edge of the forest
lay a kingdom of coldness and death.
And travellers would say that all joy drained away
when you entered that land and drew breath.

The lord of that land was King Nidud,
a man with a heart hewn of stone.
His castle was chilly and grisly and grey,
wrapped round with the wind's wild moan.

Now Nidud was cruel and greedy,
and he'd heard of the wonderful ware.
So he ordered a force of his fiercest men
to seek out the smith in his lair.

Wayland was bent at his furnace
as he worked through the dark of the night.
But the snap of a twig near his doorway
set him listening, sinews drawn tight.

He swung the door wide on its hinges
to scry out the source of the sound.
And there were the men of King Nidud
who'd circled his dwelling around.

Wayland was fierce, he was powerful.
He was built with the bulk of a bear.
He growled as three soldiers approached him,
then he lurched like a beast from his lair.

It seemed that no man could withstand him
when his temper was raised to attack.
Like skittles, those three sturdy soldiers
in amazement went staggering back.

With his strength and his wonderful weapons
he kept all those soldiers at bay.
Sheer numbers at last overcame him.
And even great Wayland gave way.

They came from all sides to constrain him.
He was wild as a beast in his rage.
But Nidud's men bound him and trussed him
and took him from there in a cage.

And they gathered his wares in a wagon,
with his furnace and anvil and gear.
They took it all back to King Nidud
in his kingdom so gaunt and so drear.

King Nidud sat high in his castle.
Wayland was brought to him there.
And though he was fastened and fettered,
still he looked strong as a bear.

So Nidud said, "Carefully, lame him.
Do nothing to damage his skill.
Sever his hamstrings to tame him,
then he'll bend to the ways of my will.

King Nidud's fair daughter, young Gunhild,
stepped forward to plead for the stranger.
But Nidud said, "Child, he is wayward and wild.
With such strength he is too great a danger."

They hacked at his hamstrings. He buckled
and fell to the floor with a groan.
"Now treat him with care," ordered Nidud,
"for this marvellous smith is my own."

A lake glistened near to the castle.
Within it a small island lay.
Beneath it King Nidud had dug a deep maze
to burrow his treasures away.

The slaves who had dug out the tunnels
were all of them slain to a man.
So no-one but Nidud and Wayland
could thread the maze through by its plan.

Above it his men made a dwelling,
and in it they put Wayland's gear.
It was there that King Nidud set Wayland to work,
to labour for year upon year.

King Nidud would cross to see Wayland
and the marvellous things he'd create.
For Wayland had nothing to do but to work,
so he laboured from early till late.

And the things that he made grew in wonder.
And they massed in the maze in a pile.
And the only thing growing yet greater
was the greed in King Nidud's grim smile.

For he thought he had tamed the wild Wayland.
Yes, he thought the great smith was his man.
But, along with his art, in the depths of his heart,
proud Wayland was hatching a plan.

Just at the brink of each daybreak
he'd limp round his isle with a sack.
The feathers he found blowing loose on the ground,
he'd secretly bring them all back.

And what did he plan for these feathers
but to fashion a pair of strong wings.
He would hide them away from King Nidud
while he charmed him with other fine things.

*   *   *

When Nidud's fair daughter, young Gunhild,
had witnessed as Wayland was lamed,
she'd seen the proud Maker reduced to a slave,
and felt herself sullied and shamed.

Whenever her father returned from his isle
with a gift of mysterious art,
she thought of the Maker, his power and his skill,
and a strange pity stirred in her heart.

And often she thought of their prisoner
and the wonderful ways of his skill.
When she pictured him there at his furnace
her blood seemed to warm with a thrill.

She thought of his animal vigour
and the fire that burned in his gaze.
She imagined his hands at their magic,
making things to enchant and amaze.

So one day she crept from the castle,
concealed in a long, hooded coat.
And under the cover of drizzle and mist,
she slipped from the shore in a boat.

She rowed herself out to the island.
When he saw her he paused from his task.
"Oh, Wayland," she said to him, shyly,
"I've come with a favour to ask."

"I've broken a beautiful buckle.
Would you mend it for me with your skill?
Perhaps I could wait here and watch you?
You will find me both quiet and still."

He let her sit near on a settle
to watch as he bent to his fire.
And the intricate play of his fingers
wove within her a web of desire.

When Wayland rose up from his furnace
for water to slake his deep thirst,
she brought up the beaker to wet his parched lips
and she thought that her young heart would burst.

And when he had drunk, she caressed him.
She stroked at his face and his hair.
She kissed at his hands and his fingers
and clung like a vine to him there.

"I must tell you," said Wayland to Gunhild,
"that my heart is bound up with my wife.
I cannot feel love for another.
I am linked to my Swan-Maid for life."

But Gunhild could bear no resistance,
and she stopped up his speech with a kiss.
She was caught in a fire of urgent desire,
and her body was eager for bliss.

And Wayland was won by her beauty
and her lovemaking quickened his lust.
He lifted her tenderly into his bed
and together they did as they must.

She knew what they did was forbidden
but often she came to him there.
She'd steal under cover of darkness or mist
to her smith in his wonderful lair.

She joyed in his animal body
and its power inside her so deep.
She would think of her Wayland, on waking,
and last thing at night, before sleep.

And Wayland did nothing to harm her,
but his heart could not open to love.
He thought of his Swan-Wife and worked on his wings
for his hope was the grey sky above.

The sons of King Nidud were warriors,
two princes both haughty and proud.
They sneaked to the island in secret one day,
knowing well it was never allowed.

They entered the forge with a swagger
and broke Wayland off from his work.
They behaved like two lords with a vassal,
and they spoke with an arrogant smirk.

"We are heirs to the throne," bragged the elder.
"We'll inherit the things that you make.
We want you to show us the treasures you store
in this hovel of yours on the lake."

The princes seemed boastful and greedy.
They were scornful and sneered at his fate.
They pressed him to show them the way through the maze
as they mimicked his shambling gait.

Now Wayland, though crippled, was powerful.
One blow could have felled them with ease.
But he wanted his plan to run smoothly,
so he shrugged at their taunts and their tease.

He showed himself patient and willing
as he led the two men through the maze.
He watched as they gaped in amazement
and he witnessed the greed in their gaze.

Said the elder, "I claim a small token,
for the hoard will be mine when I'm King."
He reached for the pile with an arrogant
 smile
and he plucked up a glittering ring.

The younger came squabbling after.

In his voice was a petulant whine.

"I too want a token to take from the pile,

for some of these things should be mine!"

"Ah, no," came the voice of the elder.

"For only the heir has that right."

"And who should decide?" quipped the younger.

"Shall we settle it here with a fight?"

The men fell to pushing and shoving.
Their greed seemed to rear like a snake.
They both drew their knives in a fury
and they fought for the hoard in the lake.

They flew at each other in anger.
They flourished their daggers with skill.
A dagger has glitter and glamour,
but the blade of a dagger can kill.

Both brothers were hot, they were hasty,
and neither was ruled by his head.
So, soon, by the cluster of treasure,
both brothers lay bloody and dead.

Wayland gazed down at the bodies.
He felt neither pity nor glee.
He'd suffered and slaved for their father
with never a thanks nor a fee.

The princes had fared him no better.
They'd shown him no care or respect.
And now, through their greed and their folly,
their own lives lay wastefully wrecked.

Wayland surveyed all his treasures,
the fruit of his spirit and art.
It seemed they'd engendered in others
only greed like a weed in the heart.

And greed will breed harshness and cruelty.
And wealth is a maze to confuse.
Once a person is warm and well-suppered,
how much of such wealth can they use?

So Wayland, he mused and he murmured,
"There's one job remains and seems right."
Then he hacked off the heads of the princes
and prepared to work into the night.

He buried the bodies quite quickly
in a pit which he dug by the hoard.
He stoked up his furnace, took both of the heads,
then he settled to work at his board.

*   *   *

With the dawn came a boat to the island,
and it brought, in a panic, the Queen.
She was seeking for news of her two missing sons.
Was there anything Wayland had seen?

Now the Queen had been heavy on Wayland.
She'd demanded so much from his skill
that sometimes it seemed all her wanting
was a coffer he never could fill.

She had never considered his comfort,
his feelings, his needs or his health.
To the Queen he was merely a maker
to add to the mass of her wealth.

So Wayland was quick to deceive her.
"They are boys. They'll be back. Never fear.
But take this small gift to your husband.
For cups should be bringers of cheer."

She gasped as she saw the two goblets.
Their work was exquisite, so fine.
"There's one for you each," whispered Wayland,
"to fill with your flowing red wine."

So the Queen took the gift back to Nidud,
leaving Wayland alone on the isle.
As she parted, he picked up a feather
and looked to the sky with a smile.

The Queen took the gift to the palace
and inspected the cups with the King.
They found that each bore fine engraving
where Wayland had pictured each thing.

The one showed their daughter with Wayland
in scenes of high sexual bliss.
King Nidud cried out in his fury,
"I'll hack out his manhood for this!"

But then they both looked at the other
and learned of the young princes' death.
They saw Wayland fashioning cups from their
    skulls,
and found they could hardly draw breath.

For the goblets were skulls clasped in silver
where Wayland had worked his best art.
But the scenes that they showed to the King and the Queen
seemed to clutch like a claw at the heart.

At the back of their minds they were guilty,
and they knew they had done Wayland wrong.
To admit such a thing was beyond them
so their tempers ran vicious and strong.

King Nidud was pallid with anger.
He gathered the best of his guard.
"We will execute Wayland," he told them.
"His death must be painful and hard."

But, as they rowed out to the island,
Wayland stood firm on the shore.
And he called out across the cold water,
"King Nidud, I serve you no more.

"The fates of your sons and your daughter
you have brought on yourself by your greed.
The treasures amassed in your pitiful maze
you may keep. Of such stuff I've no need.

"You thought to contain and control me
and to turn all my art to your gain.
But of all the fine things you have gotten,
each one is a link on a chain.

"And the chain is your love of base matter,
your longing for things and for stuff.
To finally feed such ravenous need,
no treasure is ever enough.

"But see how my art can release me
from toils and the confines of kings.
I have fashioned the means of my freedom
in the form of these wonderful wings."

Nidud looked on from the prow of the boat
and the rowers all stopped, just to stare,
as Wayland strapped into his wonderful wings
and took to the ways of the air.

"See," whispered one of the soldiers,
"The man is an angel. He flies!"
And the whole crew looked on in amazement
as they watched Wayland steadily rise.

Nidud, defeated, dropped down in the boat
and let out a world-weary sigh
as Wayland the Smith, like a bird from a cage,
flew off in the grey of the sky.

The soldiers were rapt by this marvel.
They sat in the boat and gazed on.
And there in the sky, as he flew away high,
he was joined by a beautiful swan.

The swan gave a cry, as in greeting,
and the sound seemed to ring with delight.
For a moment, just there, they wheeled in the air,
then together they flew out of sight.

It is told that they set up a forge on a hill
where he worked for the rest of his life.
And then that they flew to Valhalla,
forever as husband and wife.

And they say that the marvels he made for the maze
were gradually traded or sold,
for the pieces were all precious treasures
of metalwork, silver or gold.

So, if you should chance on some wonder
whose work seems inhumanly rare,
it may be a piece made by Wayland
who took to the ways of the air.

THE HEART SONG
OF
WAYLAND SMITH

Down on Severed Island
I ply my forge.
See how it glows,
so gold, the only light.
Late into the night I work,
turning my elvish skills
to cunning forms:
armbands, brooches, weapons, spell–ware,
all manner of metal goods
massed in a tragic pile in the maze.

Ah, but by dawn,
before the stretch and yawn
of folk who wear the day with weary habit,
the greyness cloaks my limp along the shore
to gather feathers fallen from the birds.

And see, in secret, what I fashion here:
a pair of wings to fly me up to heaven,
beyond the reach of wretched mortal toils.
So when I'm up there, hobbled as I am,
I'll fly to find my wife who flew away.

Somewhere she soars, beyond these leaden clouds,
in skies of blue where sun-rays light her face
and breezes riffle through her singing wings.

And when we meet again we'll fly together
and build a smithy high upon a ridge,
where she may have the freedom of the air
and I can make for her my finest ware.

Meanwhile on Severed Island
I ply my forge.
See how it glows, so gold,
the only light . . .

NOTE

Wayland was a legendary smith of wonderful skill whose wife was a swan-maiden, or Valkyrie, one who took the form of a swan to fly dead warriors to Valhalla, hall of the heroic dead. In the end she left him, unable to surrender her life in the air. Wayland buried himself in his work and developed a wonderful talent, always hoping to win her back. But he was captured by a greedy king, Nidud, who imprisoned him on a sunless island and forced him to make endless treasures which he had to store in a maze so intricate that only Nidud could enjoy them. Wayland escaped by making a pair of wings from feathers gathered secretly on the beach. In the legend he flew off in search of his wife. I like to imagine that he found her and that they settled at Wayland's Smithy on the Ridgeway in Berkshire (now Oxfordshire). From there she would have had instant access to the air while he could have continued to make his wonderful ware in that magical setting overlooking the Vale of the White Horse.